Big Dog and Little Dog go flying

for J.L. Hope the wind always blows strong
for you! x

EGMONT

We bring stories to life

First published in Great Britain 2006
by Egmont UK Ltd.
239 Kensington High Street, London W8 6SA
Text and illustrations copyright © Selina Young 2006
Selina Young has asserted her moral rights.
ISBN 978 1 4052 1904 4
10 9 8 7 6 5 4
A CIP catalogue record for this title is available from the British Library.
Printed in Singapore

Big Dog and Little Dog go flying

Selina Young

Blue Bananas

One hot sunny afternoon Big Dog

was walking home from town.

Big Dog had bought lots of things.

He was going to build something

amazing in his workshop.

Little Dog helped Big Dog unpack

his parcels.

Big Dog showed Little Dog how they
were going to build the aeroplane.

Big Dog got out his welding gear.

Little Dog fetched the craft box and
got out the Plasticine.

She made lots of shapes. Levers to
pull, buttons to push and knobs
to turn.

Big Dog was looking for wheels. The aeroplane needed them for take off and landing.

He rummaged around and took two wheels from a broken shopping trolley and borrowed the wheel from Little Dog's hobby horse.

Little Dog brought in all the bits she had made. But she didn't notice she had left one behind!

Big Dog fixed all the bits to the dashboard. The aeroplane was nearly finished.

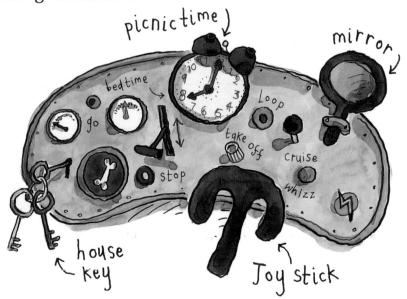

Now all Big Dog and Little Dog had
to do was paint their aeroplane.

When they had finished it was well
and truly bedtime.

Now came the exciting bit. The next day they woke up early and packed a big picnic.

They loaded all the things they
would need for their flying adventure.

They jumped in and Big Dog started the engine. The aeroplane bumped along across the garden, through the gate and down the lane.

They headed for the runway, which
was a grassy strip by the big
red barn.

Mrs Duck was there too. She was

giving her ducklings a flying lesson.

Big Dog waved happily.

20

He adjusted his goggles and pushed
the button for take off. Little Dog
hung on tight. With a pop and a bang
the aeroplane leaped into the air.

Big Dog's scarf flapped behind him

as they flew into the air.

Up in the clouds they flew past birds

and bees.

The clouds looked big and fluffy.

Big Dog said, 'Let's do some

acrobatics.' They looped the loop.

Big Dog turned a knob on the

dashboard and the aeroplane

dived down and

looped again.

Big Dog's ears flapped excitedly.

Little Dog hung on tight.

Big Dog pulled a lever and they

zoomed on towards the horizon.

They flew past some geese. Big Dog
slowed down to ask them where
would be a good place to have
a picnic.

Big Dog ran his paw along the

dashboard looking for the Landing

button. But he couldn't find it!

'We need that button to land!' said

Big Dog.

Little Dog suddenly looked

very worried.

'What are we going to do?' asked

Little Dog.

Big Dog quickly thought of a plan.

'Little Dog, you will have to

parachute home to find the button.'

'Right,' said Little Dog. 'I'll ask

Mrs Duck to fly it up to you.'

You'll be fine.

Little Dog strapped on her

parachute, trying to feel brave.

Big Dog flew back towards

their house.

Little Dog bravely leaped out of the plane, taking her umbrella for good luck. Her parachute popped open and she floated down.

Little Dog pulled on the parachute's strings and steered until she was over their own garden. Then she made a perfect landing.

She raced inside and there on the
kitchen table was the missing
Landing button.

She took the Landing button and ran
as fast as her legs would carry her to
find Mrs Duck.

Mrs Duck and the ducklings were
surprised to see her. Little Dog puffed
and panted the story and Mrs Duck
agreed to help.

Mrs Duck flapped into
the sky with the Landing
button in her beak.

She flew above the aeroplane,
wiggled her tail feathers and landed
with a plop in the back seat. Then
she handed Big Dog the button.

Thank you, Mrs Duck!

Big Dog stuck the Landing button on the dashboard and pushed it with his paw. The plane began to lower.

With a lump and a bump and a
thump Big Dog landed the plane.

Big Dog took off his goggles and leaped out of the cockpit. 'What a fantastic plane adventure!' he cried. Little Dog rushed over and hugged him.

The ducklings flapped
round quacking.

Mrs Duck led the way to a pretty

pond with a sandy spot just right

to set out a picnic.

After lunch Big Dog started drawing

in the sand.

'What are you drawing?' asked a

duckling.

'This is our next adventure!' said

Big Dog.